The Cape Cod Witch and the Pirate's Treasure

On behalf of the littlest American Thistle, who's still helping her brethren in times of need.

J Bean Palmer

Written By
J Bean Palmer

Illustrated By
Melanie Therrien

Holly Hill Press

Published in the USA by

Holly Hill Press
Post Office Box 36
East Sandwich, Massachusetts 02537

ISBN 978-1-60585-987-3

Library of Congress 2007908286
Printed in the United States of America

The Story of

ElsBeth Amelia Thistle,

Cape Cod's Youngest Witch,

And her Daring Adventure

With the Notorious Pirate

Billy Bowlegs

Dedication

This book is dedicated to those people on the Cape and Islands who make Cape Cod the magical place that it truly is.

And to Emelia, the littlest Bean, may your life always be an adventure!

Table of Contents

Chapter I
Cape Cod Massachusetts, Near the Elbow

Cape Cod Massachusetts is one of those places in the Western World that has a history, a long history. Not all of it can be explained. Perhaps, just perhaps, we'll find out that that is a good thing.

Right now all seemed idyllic here. It was another lovely fall day in this postcard-perfect Cape Cod town. Everything was quiet. Nothing unusual was happening. But was there some sort of trouble brewing just beneath this calm veneer? Was something about to happen?

Let's visit the local schoolroom and see what's up with Cape Cod's youngest witch, her school friends and the local inhabitants. Those who are magical and those who are not.

Chapter II
The Little Red Schoolhouse

El, more formally known as ElsBeth Amelia Thistle, youngest of the Cape Cod Thistles, was at this moment feeling more than a little perturbed.

Now that she was in second grade, she was discovering several things not exactly to her liking.

First of all her teacher, Ms. Finch, was a mean, old fogy. Last year ElsBeth had had the cotton-candy-sweet Mrs. Bottomley, and that had worked out just fine. But Ms. Finch was a horror. This teacher was like something out of those scary movies ElsBeth's grandmother would never let her watch.

And to make matters worse there was this annoying boy, Robert Hillman-Jones, who was absolutely driving her crazy.

The worst part of it was that ElsBeth was a witch – granted a small one – but nevertheless a broom-toting, card-carrying, bona-fide witch. ElsBeth, though only seven years old, knew several good spells, and if anyone ever deserved to be made into a frog, Robert Hillman-Jones was it. But she was not allowed to do anything about it. It was exasperating!

"Ouch!" squealed ElsBeth, as Hillman-Jones poked her ribs for the tenth time during arithmetic, the one class where Ms. Finch tolerated not the least bit of inattention. Ms. Finch went to great pains to ensure the children took arithmetic very SERIOUSLY and were ABSOLUTELY SILENT throughout.

At this unheard-of outburst, Ms. Finch turned slowly away from the blackboard, screeching the chalk for what seemed like ages. All the children held their breath as one. The teacher's beady eyes moved up under her thick glasses, black and horn rimmed, and chained to her head with multicolored plastic beads. Ms. Finch was what some people unkindly referred to as "tough on the eyes".

"What was that, Miss Thistle? Did you have something to add to today's lesson in multiplication perhaps?" Ms. Finch hissed out this question sarcastically, through her tight, thin lips.

Every child's head swung in unison in ElsBeth's direction.

"No, Ms. Finch," replied ElsBeth. But before she could stop herself, she added quietly, "Robert Hillman-Jones jabbed me in the ribs."

At this gross impertinence, Ms. Finch leapt forward at an alarming speed and swept down the row of gape-mouthed children, stopping abruptly at ElsBeth's seat. She said, "I heard that. Apologize at once. I will not have children in my class telling tales, and trying to get perfectly innocent, dear, young boys into trouble."

ElsBeth pressed her lips firmly together and sat hard on her hands so that she wouldn't say anything that would get her into further trouble - or worse yet, cast a spell in the middle of her arithmetic class.

Fortunately, at just that moment, her grandmother's unnaturally large, inky-black cat, Sylvanas, chose to make an appearance on the windowsill. The impressive feline sent a sharp, taunting hiss in Ms. Finch's direction.

The teacher, thoroughly distracted by this newest interruption to the 7's multiplication table, forgot about ElsBeth for the moment. She stepped toward the window cautiously, gingerly flapping her fingers and saying, "Scat!"

To this ridiculous effort to get him to leave, the huge cat yawned widely. He slowly arched his back, then stuck his nose in the air and plopped rather theatrically onto Amy Clark's desk.

Amy was a small timid girl with pale hair and eyes, and dressed in pink frills. She was so surprised that she started back away from her desk, and her chair tipped over into Nelson Hamm's desk in the process.

Nelson, a skinny kid with glasses, was at that moment wholly entranced by Amy in her pinkness, and was consequently completely startled. He jumped up too quickly and tried to catch Amy, but missed by a long shot, and proceeded to knock his desk into Frankie Sylvester's chair beside him.

Frankie was chunky, but he was a solid fellow, and always more than ready to get into a fight. Nelson's clumsiness called for action, and he immediately jumped up in a classic boxing stance and pushed his puny classmate over.

Unfortunately, Nelson's skinny frame presented little resistance to his classmate's powerful shove, and he flew in a slow, graceful curve - directly into Veronica Smythe.

Veronica, at that particular moment, was pleasantly day dreaming about being a teenager with make-up, hip clothes and a boyfriend. She was *not* happy to be reminded that she was still only in second grade, being bumped into by a skinny boy with glasses whose ears stuck out of the sides of his head.

Veronica let out a surprisingly loud shriek for a second grader, at which the rest of the class, as yet unaffected jumped up and began to run around in circles, thinking that a mouse must have gotten loose in the classroom. This idea was forwarded by Veronica's piercing shriek, and Carmen Alverez's cry, "Aaah! It's a mouse!"

Carmen, being deathly afraid of the little grey creatures, was always on the alert, and naturally assumed when Veronica shrieked, that she must have seen one.

The rest of the class quickly separated. Most of the boys wanted to catch the mouse and turn it into a class project. There was a group of the more squeamish girls, led by Carmen, who were squealing piercingly and jumping up on their desks to avoid the nasty rodent. A third group, consisting of several of the most serious students in the class, including ElsBeth, Lisa Lee and Johnny Twofeathers, had followed the action with alert interest as the noisy events had unfolded.

The mischievous cat was apparently satisfied that he had caused enough excitement for the moment in ElsBeth's boring arithmetic class. He plopped himself back up on the window sill and surveyed the class with a satisfied look on his feline features. He licked his chops, gave ElsBeth a slight nod and then headed off to find some other dull location in town that needed his special touch to liven things up.

ElsBeth vowed then and there that Sylvanas would be getting a large bowl of the richest cream she could find for dinner tonight. She owed him one for rescuing her from Ms. Finch's unnerving attentions.

Ms. Finch's iron control had been temporarily lost with all this chaotic behavior in her normally perfectly obedient and disciplined classroom. She was somewhat dazed even, but quickly recovered. She began to get the students back in line. The slightly confused look remaining on her face abruptly turned into a fixed glare as her sharp little eyes fell on ElsBeth, who was now smiling to herself, thinking about how wonderful Sylvanas could be.

The children sensed the sudden change in their teacher, and fell silent under Ms. Finch's completely scary look. All eyes again turned towards ElsBeth as Ms. Finch once more swept down ElsBeth's row.

"I recognized that cat. You brought him to school and called him in here. Admit it, young lady," she said.

ElsBeth wasn't sure how Ms. Finch knew that Sylvanas was a member of her family, but she managed to blurt out, "He's ours, but I didn't bring him to school."

Ms. Finch hissed back, "Don't lie to me, girl! You have Saturday detention. You will write, 'I promise not to lie, tattle or disturb the class,' on the blackboard 300 times." "Neatly!" she added, with emphasis.

At this pronouncement of punishment, Ms. Finch seemed satisfied and strode back to the blackboard.

"7 x 6 = 42
7 x 7 = 49"

She whacked the blackboard hard with the wooden pointer while pronouncing each equation crisply.

Later that afternoon as ElsBeth walked home with drooping shoulders, her eyes rarely left the sidewalk. She wasn't sure how she could stand school anymore.

Then a great idea came to her. Maybe her grandmother could take her out of school and homeschool her. She'd heard the Nye twins were being homeschooled. Not everyone had to put up with Ms. Finch. Yes! That was the answer.

Chapter III
The Garden at Six Druid Lane

With the contemplation of this much more pleasant future, ElsBeth began to cheer up. She turned down Druid Lane toward their rambling old Victorian home. And by the time she got to the front yard she was smiling again and skipping along as she usually did. ElsBeth was most usually a cheerful witch.

She soon found her grandmother out back in the herb garden. ElsBeth's grandmother was a well respected Cape Cod witch. Nevertheless, Hannah Goodspell was not an imposing figure. Plump, with fluffy grey hair pulled up into a bun and delicate wire-rimmed glasses, most people assumed she was just another helpless dear, sweet old lady. Hah!

ElsBeth, however, was well aware that Hannah Prudence Goodspell was not a witch to be trifled with.

ElsBeth was not really afraid of her grandmother. Truly she loved her grandmother to pieces. But she did respect the older witch and wanted her grandmother to always be proud of her.

The young witch hadn't decided quite how to frame today's events at school in exactly the best light so that her grandmother would have the whole picture without ElsBeth looking bad, or much worse yet, childish!

ElsBeth did not wish to be viewed as childish!

Her grandmother quickly saved her the trouble of coming up with a favorable account. "Sylvanas says you got into a bit of bother at school today."

ElsBeth could not see her grandmother's face, as Hannah was bent over the troublesome catnip patch at that moment.

"He said something about arithmetic and things being at sixes and sevens." Grandmother's ample figure began to shake. "Oh, how I love a good pun! Also, was there something about blind mice?" "Or was it blind students seeing mice?" Giggles began to erupt, and her grandmother fell over flat - right into the cabbages.

"Oh my!" she popped back up, the cabbages no worse for wear.

"Well, ElsBeth my dear, what do you have to say for yourself?" inquired Grandmother.

"I don't know who is worse, that annoying Robert Hillman-Jones or that toad Ms.

Finch." ElsBeth couldn't hold her feelings in any longer. She was kicking at the ground as if it were one of her two enemies.

Then she began to smile as she spied an enormous bullfrog. He plopped up on the garden stool and uttered a disapproving "harrumph".

"Please don't insult the honor of my close relatives. Toads may be a little slow and sometimes lack a developed sense of humor, but I'm quite sure in all my years I've never known one to be cruel," he croaked in his deep, froggy voice.

"Well, that's true enough," said ElsBeth. "But I still wanted to turn Ms. Finch into a toad."

At this, both Grandmother and Bartholomew the frog looked at her disapprovingly. Many centuries ago Bartholomew had been a handsome Indian prince named, "He Who Beats Bears" (which is its own story, for another time), but he had once made a powerful witch of his tribe terribly angry when he rejected her attentions. The witch had cast a spell on him, and he'd been a frog ever since. This was not considered a laughing matter.

ElsBeth had been quite insensitive to mention turning people into amphibians.

ElsBeth hung her head in shame. She had been carried away by her anger at school and had completely forgotten her manners.

"I'm so sorry, Bartholomew!" she cried when she realized what she had done.

Bartholomew said, "It's OK, little one. Actually, being a frog has its moments. I used to be extremely good looking as an Indian prince, but I was insufferably vain and empty-headed. A couple of centuries as a bullfrog has given me time to look at things differently. True, the first hundred years or so weren't so good. I was pretty upset and obsessed with thoughts of revenge, but the last century has been quite interesting. And my friendship with Hannah has been truly special."

At that, he smiled and hopped closer. Hannah bent down for a kiss, and for just a split second, ElsBeth saw the most handsome, tall, dark Indian brave where the bullfrog had been. She blinked, and there was familiar old Bartholomew sitting comfortably on the garden stool. ElsBeth shook her head.

Hannah Goodspell reflected that she and the bullfrog had truly become dear friends. The witch taught Bartholomew magical incantations most mornings, and Bartholomew taught her native plant lore in the afternoons. That subject contains some of the most important and necessary knowledge for a witch engaged in caring for her community.

The Goodspell witches had only come to the New World in the late 1600's. They had been well-schooled in all European plant medicinal and magical uses for many centuries. But the New World was different, and this knowledge had to be gained bit by bit. It certainly was helpful to have the friendship of a former Indian prince whose tribal knowledge dated back millennia to get a leg up on understanding the local flora in all its important uses.

These pleasant musings were soon inter-rupted by Sylvanas, who had been missing during the earlier conversation. The huge cat made a typically grand entrance, appearing out of thin air and landing solidly (as he was a little overweight), but with an impressive theatrical pose, right beside Bartholomew on the garden stool.

Hannah Goodspell looked into his brilliant green eyes and knew he was up to something once again.

"What is it, Sir? You look like the cat that ate the cream." Despite the trouble he frequently caused, Sylvanas never failed to be interesting, and he was an incorrigible gossip.

The cat purred "Yes. I've got a surprise lined up for that prune-faced teacher. I do believe that the boys in the class will be unusually pleased tomorrow."

Ignoring all the questions from ElsBeth, Bartholomew and Hannah, the cat would say no more of his plans. He struck a new pose, looking like a statue of the sphinx, and remained mum and completely mysterious. (He loved doing this.)

Grandmother finally ended the pleading by saying, "It is no use. He's made up his mind. Let's go in. I have an apple pie in the oven, which should be done now. I made some beach plum ice cream for dessert. And we have some tasty Cape Cod witch's stew to start." She cackled good naturedly at this announcement, and everyone headed inside, except the frog who could not eat that kind of food anymore - much to his regret.

Chapter IV
A Typical Evening for the Witches

ElsBeth loved her grandmother's witch's stew, a mixture of fresh tomatoes, vegetables and spices from the garden, smothered in three-cheese sauce. It was always accompanied by anadama bread fresh from the oven. (For those of you who have never had anadama bread fresh from the oven, you are missing a favorite New England treat made with cornmeal and molasses, and one that smells *most* wonderful while baking.)

With a full belly after the last course of hot apple pie and the homemade ice cream - a special favorite of Sylvanas - ElsBeth got to her most important studies. Being a witch was a huge responsibility and required daily study and practice. And a lot of patience.

She had been working for the last weeks on mastering a protective spell for a small kitchen garden. This was a fundamental skill for any witch worthy of the name. She had been practicing on yard-long squares of the garden that her grandmother had marked off with twine. She was now on her fifth square. ElsBeth would have to admit that the first two squares were a poor show, looking brown at the edges and wilty. She could hear faint weepy sounds coming from those sections. The poor plants there were sadly embarrassed about their withered appearance.

However, each of the last three squares looked progressively greener and plumper. And now there was a perfect tomato growing very fast in front of her eyes. "Eureka!" she squealed in delight, "I've got the hang of it!"

Her grandmother popped out the back door to see what all the noise was about. She folded her arms and beamed at her granddaughter. ElsBeth was a little impatient and had too much of a temper, but she was doing all right. Hannah decided that the littlest Cape Cod witch was coming along just fine.

Chapter V
Dreams of Pirates and Treasure

That night in her small captain's bed, ElsBeth had dreams. She rarely had dreams, but tonight her dreams seemed almost realer than real.

There was a pirate. He was short and had bowed legs, and there was a cave and gold and jewels and swords and some men skulking around. And then there was Robert Hillman-Jones, tied up and looking scared and very cold.

What was Robert Hillman-Jones doing in her dream? It was bad enough she had to put up with him during the day. "Oh well," she sighed and went back into a deep slumber until the bright morning sun woke her up.

At breakfast her grandmother gave ElsBeth a long serious look. "ElsBeth, did you have a dream last night?" she inquired.

ElsBeth, surprised by the question, replied, "Yes, I did, Grandmother!"

"Was it about pirates?" Hannah queried.

"Why, yes, it was." ElsBeth was even more surprised.

"We haven't talked about this yet, but tonight instead of your usual lessons, we will cover a new topic. Witch's dreams often have special meanings. But enough for now, you'll be late for school if you don't get out the door, young lady."

ElsBeth looked to the tall, moon-faced grandfather's clock in the hall, who promptly winked right back at her. She grabbed her half-eaten, cranberry-pumpkin-nut muffin, and her pack, and dashed out the door.

Calling, "See you tonight, Grandmother. I love you," ElsBeth was off.

Chapter VI
Not Just Another Day of School

ElsBeth waited with the other children in the school yard for the bell. The boys seemed particularly obnoxious and secretive today, whispering in a huddled group by the climbing structure. ElsBeth and the other girls wondered what they were up to, but their speculations were cut short by the start-of-school bell.

Ms. Finch's class settled quickly in their seats. She did not put up with tardiness or fooling around. That was for sure!

Ms. Finch cleared her throat significantly and said, "Well, children, instead of spelling, this morning we are going to take up history. We will be preparing a special Halloween pageant this year, and the School Board in its infinite wisdom has decided that the time spent can count toward your history lessons." Ms. Finch spat this last part out as if she didn't think too much of the School Board, Halloween, or taking credits for this as part of history class!

"Now, you children probably know nothing about the history of Halloween," pronounced Ms. Finch in her "I-am-so-much-older-and-smarter-than-you" voice. "So I am going to give you an assignment to ask your parents - or in the case of two of our students who don't seem to have any parents" (and at this she looked pointedly at ElsBeth and Johnny Twofeathers), "you must ask your grandparents. You are to have them explain to you all about the celebration of Halloween. Then you are to write a short essay on the subject with NO spelling errors and NEAT penmanship. And there are to be no marks outside the lines or you must write it over and over again until you get it right. Am I COMPLETELY understood?"

"Any questions?" She paused for a mere fraction of a second - to ensure no one had time to raise a hand - and plunged on.

"Now, as to the pageant itself, we have costumes from the previous years in the closet. There should be enough for each child. One of you boys," Ms. Finch's eagle gaze surveyed the room and landed on poor Nelson, "Nelson Hamm…"

Nelson looked up nervously from staring at Amy Clark's blond curls.

"Go get the costumes and pass them out," commanded Ms. Finch.

If anyone at that moment had happened to look at the window sill, they would have noticed an imposing, green-eyed, black cat, who appeared to be eagerly awaiting something.

Nelson's protruding ears turned bright red as he reluctantly rose from his small desk and shuffled to the classroom storage closet. The door stuck, and Nelson had to yank it hard. Suddenly the door swung wide and hundreds and hundreds of noisy little brown mice began pouring out into the classroom, squeaking excitedly at the top of their little lungs.

Carmen Alverez promptly began screaming hysterically, "Mice! Mice!" The frantic girl started running in fast circles around her desk, while at the same time trying to jump up on it.

At this signal all the children, even the toughest boys, began hopping up onto their desks and jumping up and down screaming.

Sylvanas was comfortably seated on the window sill, which was a wonderful vantage point, and looked on with great satisfaction at the lovely, ensuing chaos.

ElsBeth was at first amused, but quickly began to be worried that some poor mouse would be tromped on with all the jumping around being done. As the only witch present, she felt responsible for the little creatures.

Ms. Finch had hopped up on her desk, too, and was glaring down at the mice. But then her eyes swept across the room and like a laser aimed straight at ElsBeth.

"ElsBeth, I know you have somehow managed to get those mice in here. You are in Big Trouble, young lady. Get them out. NOW!" she shouted.

ElsBeth decided that this was not the time to protest her innocence. She needed to get these creatures safely outside. She couldn't use a spell, but she could easily speak to them in their own squeaky language, having had many conversations with the little brown fluff balls during her seven years. So, quietly squeaking instructions, she led the excited little ones out the classroom door, through the wide hallway, and down the front steps, as quickly as could be.

The school's principal, Dr.Titcomb, poked his head out his office door, right as the floating carpet of mice was heading out the front. He shook his handsome silver hair and blinked several times, but by then they were gone. He looked down the hall toward Ms.

Finch's door, and then headed back towards his desk, thumbs in suspenders, thoughtfully muttering something about "having to lay off the Scotch at happy hour over at the Dan'l Webster Inn."

As ElsBeth was leading them outside, she heard several of the mice excitedly mentioning Sylvanas' name. ElsBeth looked around for her friend, but the cat was long gone - no doubt bored with school, now that the initial excitement was over.

When she returned, the classroom had begun to settle down. The children were seated once again, and Ms. Finch had regained the floor and begun pacing the aisles. The children looked uneasy. You never knew with Ms. Finch.

"Nelson Hamm, I said pass out the costumes," she now repeated through clenched teeth.

Poor Nelson, who had been shaking behind the closet door unnoticed since the flood of mice began, jumped back into the closet and grabbed an armful of costumes. He hastily dropped one at each desk as he went around the room.

There was a goblin, an elf, a witch, a pirate, some Indians, a cat, a frog, a turkey, a mouse, a bat, several Pilgrims, a sea captain, a cowboy, a princess and a few costumes for which the identity could only be guessed.

A certain amount of excitement was generated as each student looked over his or her costume, despite Ms. Finch's unrelenting glare.

The rest of the morning was spent trying them on and practicing the various scenes Ms. Finch had designed to make up the pageant.

ElsBeth was pleased to note that Robert Hillman-Jones was a pirate, just like in her dream. Well — not precisely like in her dream. In her dream he was a scared little boy. But there was a pirate involved. That was for certain!

In the classroom there was a lot of grumbling by those who felt their costume was not exactly what they would want to be for Halloween, but most of that was done in whispers. No one wanted to set Ms. Finch off again.

ElsBeth was a bat, which was perfect! ElsBeth's favorite creatures were bats.

People often had funny ideas that bats were scary and sucked your blood and turned you into a vampire. But that was silly. Bats are actually sweet, intelligent creatures, and the reason they fly close to you in the evening is to keep the mosquitoes and other pesky bugs away. Of course, bats think mosquitoes are delicious, a taste ElsBeth could not quite understand. But as Grandmother often said, "To each his own."

Unknown to her classmates, ElsBeth had a familiar. A witch's familiar is the one creature, special to that particular witch, who would always help the witch no matter what happened. ElsBeth's own familiar was a bat. His name was Professor Badinoff, and he was extremely intelligent. He was a large bat and imposing, but with delicate pointed ears and a refined, aristocratic bearing. Many of the other creatures on the Cape thought Badinoff was an intellectual snob, but secretly they were proud to have someone so incredibly sophisticated and world-renowned for his encyclopedic knowledge as part of their small rural community.

On the weekends Professor Badinoff helped ElsBeth with multiplication, a skill which was not coming easily to her. Perhaps this was because Ms. Finch's lessons were boring, stupid and somewhat disturbing with all the loud thwacking of her pointer against the blackboard!

Now, not everyone knows that all witches have a witch's mark. It is always in the shape of their familiar, so that no matter what happened, even if they lost their memory, they would always be reminded of the one creature who could help them the most in any situation.

This is not the same type of mark that was referred to in the ridiculous Salem witch stories. Her grandmother had been quick to point this out. Those poor girls were quite ordinary individuals with just a common mole or a birthmark. They unfortunately took the brunt of the evil gossips of Salem, back long ago.

ElsBeth, however, as a real witch, had the cutest little brown bat mark on the bottom of her left heel. It was tiny, but if one looked closely, it was clearly seen as a bat with outstretched wings.

So, ElsBeth was perfectly happy to be a bat.

Veronica, however, took one look at ElsBeth's costume and said, "El, yuck! You have to be a bat! Look at me. I'm an Indian princess."

At that, Veronica struck a pose and fluffed her feather headdress dramatically.

ElsBeth stuck out her chin and said defensively, "What's wrong with being a bat?"

Johnny Twofeathers, dressed incongruously as a Pilgrim, slid over and pulled ElsBeth away from Veronica. "Shush! Ms. Finch has it in for you. Don't start anything or you'll be in detention all week."

ElsBeth struggled to keep her temper under control. She just couldn't stand it when people said bad things about bats! But finally good sense won out, and she smiled at Johnny and said, "Thanks, Chief!" Johnny was the eldest grandson of a Wampanoag leader, and ElsBeth knew he would be Chief someday. She had known him forever and always called him that ever since she could talk, though no one else did.

Ms. Finch, seeming to have forgotten all the distractions by now, began to arrange the children. The pageant was to be held the Saturday after next, right before Halloween. The parents and the whole town would be invited, and then following the pageant there was to be a huge Halloween celebration in the auditorium with candy, apple bobbing, a haunted house, a pumpkin carving contest, fortune telling - the works. The other classes were preparing the decorations, but the second graders were to be the stars of the show.

The teacher worked on each grouping for the pageant – the animals, the Pilgrims, the Indians and the mystical creatures. She had them practice stopping in a clever "tableau", (Ms. Finch loved saying the word "tableau" which means "a living picture". She learned this at her teacher's retreat last summer and used it every chance she could. Ms. Finch had secret hopes of eventually becoming the drama teacher at the High School when Mortimer Hicks retired someday. (But that is another story, too.)

Ms. Finch then had the children practice turning toward the imaginary audience with a little bow and marching on in a dignified fashion. That is, Ms. Finch *hoped* it would eventually look dignified. That was going to take a lot of work, Ms. Finch considered, but she gritted her teeth and pressed her thin lips together in firm determination to make it so. She was set on having an "artistically significant" pageant, no matter what!

After about an hour of serious drilling, the children did actually look somewhat stately. But with all this dignified classroom behavior, the mischievous nature of Sylvanas had again been aroused. The cat had become bored - always a dangerous situation with Sylvanas - and he decided that the moment had arrived for him to introduce some more fun. He felt that the children should have an opportunity to make this Halloween rehearsal something to be remembered. Perched on the schoolhouse window, he watched Ms. Finch position the children carefully once again, and then begin to move them along in their solemn progression.

With a wink of one large green eye, the windows along the far wall opened wide, and the ever-ready trickster, the North Wind, suddenly swept through the room at gale force. Hats and masks flew off amid shrieks. Ms Finch's glasses somehow blew off her head, and then blew right back onto her nose, precisely upside down. Her short black hair stuck straight up in the air. After swirling briefly through the excited children, the wind homed in on the helpless teacher. He swirled around her for several tense minutes in closer and closer circles. Ms. Finch tried to escape by hopping here and there, but wherever she went, the whirling wind followed her. She began to hop frantically, like a crazy cross between a giant bunny and an African Whatusi dancer. The children stared amazed.

ElsBeth happened to look over at the window just then and did a double take. Sylvanas, normally the most aloof and condescending of creatures, was laughing hysterically. In his case this most resembled a small panther trying to cough up a giant hairball.

Finally, exhausted, Ms. Finch crawled underneath her desk, and the devilish North Wind, unable to maintain the momentum, got tired of the game and left. As did the cat, greatly satisfied with his day's "school work" and still chuckling softly to himself.

The rest of the day was comparatively quiet and ended up with things pretty much back to normal by three o'clock.

Finally the bell rang for end of school. All the children loitered outside afterward, as if there were yet some unfinished business.

Veronica was stroking her stylish brown locks. Johnny Twofeathers was looking like what he was, a small Indian chief – very wise and very still.

41

Amy Clark was still a bit fearful. Actually, she always was. She was looking nervously at her toes. Nelson Hamm was looking nervously at Amy Clark. Frankie Sylvester was looking for someone to intimidate. And Carmen Alverez was carefully looking around for any mice that might still be present.

Robert Hillman-Jones swaggered out the door last, swinging his back pack up, and coolly announced, "Men, it's *Showtime!*"

Most of the girls rolled their eyes to the top of their heads thinking, "Oh my goodness, what are they up to now?"

The boys crowded toward the big apple tree in the corner of the school yard. Frankie Sylvester climbed up as high as he could without breaking any branches. As his mother frequently asserted, "Frankie was big-boned," so he only got about halfway up before dangerous creaking sounds warned him not to go further. He was lookout. Someone had to ensure no girls, or heaven forbid, younger boys, heard the plan or had a chance to get in on the action.

The girls, truth be told, were not actually very interested in what the boys were doing and began to drift off toward home either by themselves or with a best friend. Little did they know they would later have reason to regret being so incurious about the boys' plans.

Chapter VII
Fairy Stories

ElsBeth was especially excited to get home that evening. She wasn't sure if her grandmother would approve of Sylvanas' escapades, so she decided better not to bring it up. It would be good to have the cat's actions unrestricted by grandmother's possible prohibition, just in case Ms. Finch got to be too much again.

ElsBeth felt sure the mischievous cat could be counted on to create a classroom disturbance anytime Ms. Finch started picking on her too badly.

With that moral question settled, she headed down the long, crushed shell drive, shaded on each side by tall oaks and pine trees. She soon reached her grandmother's comfortable old house, trimmed in shades of pink and lavender and looking out over the river and marsh onto the mighty Atlantic Ocean to the east.

"Grandmother, Grandmother, I'm home!" she shouted as she skipped up the front porch steps. Boy, the house smelled inviting with hot mulled cider simmering on the back of the wood stove. The scent of the spices - cinnamon, nutmeg, cloves and ginger - momentarily swept away all thought of the adventures of the day. ElsBeth helped herself to a small cup of her favorite drink.

She breathed deeply the heavenly brew as she poured it into her very own witch's mug, which was shaped like a brown bat with his wings touching in back. She curled up in a huge, old, wicker rocking chair on the side porch and looked out at the garden.

Grandmother's rather ample behind popped up next to a large fennel plant where she was removing some strawberry runners that had strayed from their patch. ElsBeth knew well that witches had to spend a lot of time in their gardens because plants are so important in a witch's repertoire. ElsBeth would usually find her grandmother there when she wasn't out and about on other magical errands.

"I'll join you in a minute, dear." Hannah neatly grabbed up all her gardening tools and said her goodbye to Prince Bartholomew, who had been keeping her company and giving excellent advice on the care of several native herbs.

After cleaning up, Hannah poured some of the spicy cider into her mug - hers was shaped like a large bullfrog with an amazing resemblance to Bartholomew - and she joined ElsBeth on the porch.

"Well, young lady, was school any better today?"

ElsBeth's considered reply was, "It was very interesting."

Her grandmother looked askance at ElsBeth's answer but said nothing. She just smiled wisely.

ElsBeth remembered her assignment. "We need to write an essay about Halloween and I'm supposed to ask you about it."

Hannah leaned back and began in her teaching voice. "Halloween is the most special holiday for witches. It has been celebrated for at least two thousand years and probably much longer. 'Halloween' means Holy Evening, and it is always at the end of summer. Many believe it was started in Ireland and Britain. And instead of pumpkins - turnips and beets were carved there and were lit with candles. It is a time when the barriers between the natural world and the supernatural world are weak or broken.

"Halloween is the most powerful magical time of the year. The lanterns are carved to help the ghosts of loved ones to find their way home, or to scare the bad ones away with a spooky carving if they mean ill. Traditionally, large bonfires are set, to keep the evil spirits away.

"In these times, in most of America, it is just a time for children to dress up and create mischief and get candy. But here on Cape Cod, the holiday is still important to many people. Even non-witches here get a little fey, and are apt to see ghosts and goblins, though few would ever admit it. To those who are receptive, the future often becomes clear.

"Best of all, the few fairies who made it to America will sometimes let themselves be seen."

"Wow, Grandmother, I've never seen a fairy," piped up ElsBeth at this startling information.

Hannah looked dreamily into the sunset and began to cast her mind back. "It was 1666. I was newly arrived to this continent, having been sent for by your grandfather, a promising but rebellious warlock who had been dispatched to the New World earlier - since he kept causing too much trouble in the old country, Oh, he was a feisty one," she added with a smile. "Our ship had landed at Boston Harbor safely, despite the rough seas that by all rights should have capsized us not long out of England. Fortunately, there were several witches aboard, and between us we were able to cast spells effective enough to keep our small craft afloat on the giant ocean swells.

"Your grandfather was anxious when he met the ship with his small pony cart. He had sensed the rough seas in the Atlantic for the last weeks. You see, we'd been betrothed for many years – since we could barely form our first spells – and we remained close in spirit, no matter how far the physical distance.

"He was so excited to see me again after all these years of separation. We would finally be able to start our lives together. I shyly climbed up beside his handsome figure, while he safely stowed my few belongings that hadn't been lost overboard in the storms. I had one large brocade bag filled with odds and ends given us by our relatives - things that were meant to help us get started in the colony.

"We were on a rough road headed out of Boston, when I heard a strange squeaky noise. It seemed to be coming from the brocade bag. I assumed a frightened mouse had somehow gotten trapped inside, and I hastened to let the poor little creature out. When I opened the bag, however, the squeaking stopped abruptly, and a small scratching noise started up. I began to move things around to get at the source of the sounds.

"Aunt Eulaylia had sent over a small silver chest as a wedding present, cautioning me not to open it until my wedding day. Well, that very day was to be my wedding day. Nathaniel and I were to be married as soon as we got to Salem. The small community of witches there would conduct the ceremony and host our wedding night. But the scratching got so insistent, I forgot all due caution and just opened up the ornate, jeweled silver box without a thought. And what do you suppose was inside?"

"I don't know, Grandmother. What?" ElsBeth was completely entranced.

"The maddest, tiniest pair of fairies you ever laid you eyes on. That's what!

"Aunt Eulaylia felt sorry for us being in the New World without any fairies to keep us company, so she had enchanted a young fairy couple that her cat, Lord Farthingales, had captured. She cast a spell on them so they would sleep through the journey, and then with the utmost care, she placed them in the silver box, which had been lined in plush red velvet so they would slumber in complete comfort on the long, dangerous sail across the sea. They had now awoken from their long enchantment and were VERY displeased with the state of affairs.

"Fairies have terrible tempers when provoked," she added, shaking her head at the memory.

"I can tell you my heart was in my throat. If we hadn't kept that Pilgrim ship afloat, those two potent beings might have been lost to the world, or worse yet, captured by Neptune who has more than enough magic horsepower already, thank you very much!

"When I looked closely at them, I saw the most perfect, delicate creatures with pink and purple wings – like little hummingbirds, but as I said, the effect was spoiled when they opened their little rosebud lips. The words that came out of those two would make an old sailor blush to his toes. And their voices - they would pierce your ears. And they had steely sharp, little teeth, too.

"Nathaniel and I were so surprised that we forgot to clamp down on the lid right away, and with a gleeful, high pitched laugh and several dirty taunts, they flew close to our noses once, then twice, and were off.

"On each of their perfect, tiny faces there had been an expression of smug triumph. They had escaped a powerful enchantment after all. Before they left, they had taken time to give us a good look over. They were sneering a little, so they probably thought we were a bit wet behind the ears. But they seemed to accept us. After all, witches are magical cousins to all fairies, as well as elves and goblins. Mostly, I'm sure they were happy to be free of any spell or obligation to us, which would have been the case had we been just a hair quicker.

"The only other time I've ever seen a fairy, since leaving the old country, was just before the Salem witch trials. Nathaniel and I were fast asleep on our farm after dusk. It was the night of the full moon and the orb was rising huge and pumpkin colored in the sky, as it often does on crisp fall evenings in this part of the world. We were suddenly awakened by a quiet, almost imperceptible, but insistent, tapping at the window.

"Nathaniel got up and could see a small blur outside. We didn't have windows you could open in those days, so he donned a robe and ran out to find out what it was. He

53

had hardly opened the door when the very same two fairies buzzed his ears. They warned him that we had to leave Salem that night, and told us where we must go.

"Fairies aren't generally very thoughtful creatures. In fact, they are usually tricksters and can't be trusted at all. But it seemed they hadn't found much in the way of magic in the New World, so they had apparently decided to adopt us to protect what little magic there was. Nathaniel and I were a significant portion of the local magical community back in those days. Nathaniel quickly told them where the other witches could be found so they could be saved, too. And the tiny beings were off in a wink, leaving a small trail of gold glitter across the cold night sky in their wake.

"Nathaniel and I packed up our pony cart, awakened Sylvanas, who was still deep asleep by the hearth - he's always been an unnaturally sound sleeper. We gathered up the treasures I had brought from Ireland, and within the half-hour, we were heading south for Cape Cod, and away from those dreadful witch trials.

"I've never seen those fairies or any others since that night, at least not directly. But

they surely are around. One sees the signs
now and then.

"Well ElsBeth, you certainly got me going.
Halloween is a great tradition and I'm glad to
hear your teacher is having you learn of it."

ElsBeth prickled a bit at the idea of praise
for her arch enemy Ms. Finch, but perhaps
Grandmother was right. Ms Finch couldn't
be all bad. And the pageant was sure to be
fun, as well as the party with all the treats
and apple bobbing and pumpkin carvings
and the haunted house!

Her mind was busy imagining all these
delights when Grandmother brought her
back to earth. "It's time to peel the
vegetables and get supper on the table.
Come into the kitchen and help please,
ElsBeth." Even witches have to do chores.

Tonight's dinner was especially delicious,
with leak soup, and cabbages stuffed with
tomatoes, herbs, and savory cheeses. The
crusty bread was straight from the oven, and
there was fresh butter from Farmer Green's
lovely cow Beatrice. And for dessert there was
cranberry-black walnut torte with whipped
cream!

Grandmother told ElsBeth often that she was lucky to be a witch. "Regular children often had to eat fast food, which is an abomination and not natural at all!" She always shook her head sadly after she said this.

ElsBeth decided that some day she would learn to cook as well as her grandmother. Cooking was an important skill for a witch. It was hard to cast a decent spell on an empty stomach, and witches, and even regular mortals, did best with tasty, nutritious meals inside their bellies.

After dinner they settled in by the fireplace. The days were starting to cool off, and there was a chill to the evening. Grandmother and ElsBeth sat in the plump cushions of the large wing chairs and sipped their hot chocolates. Soon Grandmother began to speak of dreams. "Part of being a witch is knowing what the future is likely to hold. If you have some warning, you can often influence events for the better and even sometimes prevent a tragedy.

"No witch can completely control the future, but many have had a strong influence for good...or evil," she added ominously. Grandmother almost whispered these last words. She shook herself a little as if casting off a bad memory.

"ElsBeth, dreams often tell us something we wouldn't otherwise know about the future. When the body rests, the spirit is sometimes free to roam about in the world. You may also piece together bits of things you observed during the day, and sometimes from even weeks before. You may reach some conclusion you would not otherwise ever have come to realize. We witches do not often dream, but when we do it is important.

"And I'm worried about the dream you had. There have been other signs that some evil is about nearby. And it is almost Halloween, a time when the spirit world and the everyday world are much more closely connected then usual. We must pay attention. I fear that something quite disastrous may happen if we are not alert.

"Tonight I'm giving you your own diary. If you dream again, the moment you awaken you must write everything down immediately. No matter how silly it may seem at the time, it may help to avoid a terrible tragedy in the future."

With that auspicious warning, Hannah handed ElsBeth a purple, leather-bound journal with lined pages and a lavender, velvet ribbon to mark the place. A small silver bat weighted the end of the ribbon. ElsBeth felt very grave that her grandmother would think her dreams so important, and she clutched her diary to her small body. "I understand. I promise I'll write everything the minute I wake up."

That night, wrapped in a pink flannel nightgown embroidered with tiny brown bats, the young witch slept deeply. But there were no dreams.

Chapter VIII
Back to School

School went on for the next week and an half with the excitement building as the children, teachers and even the parents began to prepare for the Halloween pageant and party. The ordinary had to be endured, though. Multiplication tables were practiced, spelling lessons were learned. Reading classes were sweated through by many of the children.

In this Ms. Finch was very particular about e-nun-ci-a-tion. Poor Nelson Hamm never liked to be called upon and had a slight stutter anyway. Reading aloud, with Ms. Finch interrupting at each hesitation, mispronunciation or stumble, was a nerve-wracking experience, and dreaded by most.

ElsBeth fortunately was a good reader. Her grandmother had read to her ever since she was a tiny baby. Witches don't believe in watching TV- there is too much to do in the real world! So books were the main diversion, once chores and lessons were done, of course.

From age four, ElsBeth had liked to read with her own voice. Witches all love the sound of their own voices. Her grandmother had been very patient as ElsBeth had stumbled her way through the words at first. Because she had never been interrupted or criticized, she had turned into a natural and fluent reader. And because she was a witch, she had an uncanny ability to imitate animals and people. If anything, ElsBeth always had to restrain herself from being too realistic in her renditions of the reading assignments. Ms. Finch required precision - but emotion and drama were just not allowed.

Aside from the occasional traumatic reading experience by one or the other of the students, the only thing of note during this time happened in the special pumpkin carving class. They had art class once per week, and instead of the usual finger painting, leaf tracing or ceramic palm print ashtrays, Ms. Finch was allowing a special pumpkin carving class. She especially wanted to monitor this pumpkin carving activity herself.

A lot was at stake. There was to be a huge lobster trap filled with candy, donated by the Penny Candy Store in Centerville, as the prize for the best carving.

The children soon learned that Ms. Finch was deathly opposed to cheating - there was at least one lecture a day on the subject. This meant that help from brothers, sisters and parents was strictly forbidden. Just yesterday Ms. Finch had proclaimed authoritatively that "All children are natural cheaters!" and then she had added under her breath, "and worse."

At this, the children had looked around suspiciously at each other. They hadn't realized they were all cheaters, though for sure Veronica had intended to ask her mother, a well known Cape Cod sculptress, to help her with her carving.

Ms. Finch had ordered each child to bring in their own pumpkin of no greater than ten inches in diameter, and they would do the tracing and carving under her strict supervision.

On the carving day, each student had to line their desk with layers of old newspaper. Pumpkin carving is well known to be extremely messy. An apron of some sort had to be brought from home. And there was quite a variety to be found amongst the classmates.

Amy had a frilly pink thing just her size. Nelson had a large red one with "Baste Me" in big black letters on it. Jimmy, whose father was a local lobster fisherman, had a highly effective old yellow slicker, though it exuded a slightly fishy smell. Lisa Lee had a faded picture of Albert Einstein covered over with complicated mathematical formulas on hers. Veronica wore something artful with embroidered butterflies floating around on it amidst graceful, green dragonflies, no doubt purchased at great expense from one of the trendy Chatham shops. ElsBeth had on one of her grandmother's aprons, decorated with beautiful green and gold rainforest frogs.

All the students were well armed with identical tools - orange plastic pumpkin carving implements and black magic markers.

After the daily lectures on cheating, only Robert Hillman-Jones had the nerve to attempt such an unadmirable thing. He had brought a *Family Circle* magazine pumpkin carving pattern to trace, and kept referring to it sneakily under the table.

Several of the carvings done by the class turned out to be minor works of art. ElsBeth made a beautiful bat with a lopsided smile and big ears. Veronica made a sprightly goblin that had a surprising resemblance to Johnny Depp. No doubt her mother wasn't the only talented one in the family. Jimmy made a lobster, which was a new twist on Halloween, but he pulled it off by making it extremely scary. Lisa Lee had taken a perfectly symmetrical pumpkin and had precisely carved her hero, Albert Einstein, doing a great job on his hair. No one quite knew what Nelson Hamm's carving was. Some thought it was a rat but several thought it was a Salvador Dali style werewolf. It definitely sparked the greatest debate and at least one fist fight when Frankie Sylvester defended his interpretation to Jimmy Miller. Johnny Twofeathers made an osprey – an eagle-like bird well loved on the Cape. Amy made a kitten.

After keeping his carving carefully hidden under newspaper the whole time, finally, at the end of class, Robert Hillman-Jones revealed his creation. It was carved on an extremely squat, rare, white pumpkin that everyone swore was not within the ten inch limit. It was incredibly ornate with a half moon, a witch on a broom, a cat and curlicues of ivy, laced intricately around the back and sides.

The children stood gape-mouthed with indrawn breaths. Everyone had seen him referring to the tracing paper hidden in his lap. As one, they looked up for Ms. Finch's terrible reaction to his blatant cheating.

Ms. Finch walked slowly over to Hillman-Jones's desk, and Robert smiled up meltingly

at her pinched face. Suddenly a beatific
smile broke through on her normally severe
features and she actually giggled girlishly.
"Well, I'm not sure what the other classes
have come up with, but this is certainly the
most impressive carving I've seen in the long
history of Mid Cape Elementary School. Well
done Mr. Hillman-Jones! Well done, I say!"

ElsBeth was steaming. How could eagle
eye Finch not know he cheated? Veronica's
pumpkin should have won hands down if it
weren't for Hillman-Jones' treachery.

ElsBeth was about to burst forth with a
hasty accusation that surely would have
gotten her another long Saturday detention,
when she felt Johnny Twofeathers' arm on
hers. "Don't do it," he whispered. "She just
wants him to win. If you say anything, he'll
still win but you'll be in big trouble. It's
Halloween. You don't want detention now."
At those wise words, ElsBeth deflated like an
old balloon. Johnny was right, and very
brave to risk whispering in Ms. Finch's class -
Ms. Finch was especially death on
whispering. ElsBeth had to let it go.

Later when the school bell rang, the boys
made a beeline for the apple tree. Whatever
scheme they had been working on the last

few weeks seemed to be coming close to fruition.

ElsBeth and the other girls speculated about what the boys were up to. It was broadly agreed that they were either planning a major toilet papering of the town, or would try to climb the church bell tower and leave some obnoxious sign. It would be somewhat brave and mildly entertaining, but the girls really didn't expect too much. Naive girls!

Chapter IX
Halloween - The Big Day

And so the days went by. Right up to
Halloween. Halloween fell on a Saturday this
year, which was wonderful. The children
would have all day to set up the auditorium
with the decorations, including the best
haunted house ever. It even had small rooms
where you could thrust your arm through a
curtain to feel around. There would be bowls
of peeled grapes for eyeballs and cold
spaghetti for brains. It was going to be really
gross and spooky, especially with Mr. Spark's
special effects. Mr. Sparks used to work in
Hollywood for Steven Spielberg, but it was
whispered around town that he'd had a
"meltdown", and was back on Cape Cod
recovering far away from that "viper's nest" in
Los Angeles, California.

He seemed pretty well to the children. He
was a bit skittish, but he loved creating scary
lighting effects that only came on when
someone was about to walk by. Between Mr.
Sparks and Veronica's mother, who made the
ghosts and witches that would pop up, it
seemed like this would be the best Halloween
celebration ever held in this small Cape Cod
town.

The children and parents began drifting in
about 7:30 on the morning of the big day.
Around 9:30 it became obvious that
something was missing. Or more accurately

some*ones* were missing. There was not a
second grade boy there. Nelson Hamm's
father was the first to notice it and mention
something. "Say, my boy took off early this
morning and said he'd meet us here. That
was almost three hours ago." Soon, several
other parents were saying much the same
thing. The boys had all taken off early and
not been seen since.

It was assumed by the adults that there
was some Halloween prank in the offing, and
no one got too worried until lunchtime rolled
around with no word. None of the boys were
known to have taken any food with them, and
several were notorious for not going more
than an hour without whining about being
"completely starving" and begging for food.

Finally at 12:05 one of the parents,
Frankie Sylvester's dad, who was also the
Town Constable, stepped slowly up on the
stage. He had a firm jaw and was tall and
broad. Constable Sylvester was someone
everyone in town knew and respected. He
called out calmly in his low policeman's voice,
"Now folks, gather round please. It seems like
several of our boys from the second grade
class are missing. I'm sure it is nothing to
worry about. Boys that age like to pull
pranks, especially on Halloween. I know I did
when I was that age," he added, and a few

people chuckled. "But they've been gone longer than they should, so we ought to set about finding them. Does anyone have any idea where these kids could have gone?"

The auditorium broke out in nervous whispers until Veronica Smythe stuck up a small insistent arm. "Constable Sylvester, we've noticed the boys planning something for weeks."

The Constable thanked her gently and inquired, "Did any of you children overhear anything about what they were planning?"

Carmen Alverez spoke up, "We couldn't, Frankie was lookout and wouldn't let anyone near enough to hear anything." Carmen stopped abruptly when she realized it was Frankie's dad she was reporting to.

Constable Sylvester cleared his throat loudly and said, "Thank you, Carmen."

No one else had anything more to say, so the Constable announced, "Well, it looks like we are going to need a search party. Those boys could only have gone on bicycles and it's only been a few hours. They can't be far. We'll break up into groups, each with a leader. You children stay here and continue with the Halloween party preparations. We don't want to have to search for anyone else. We'll find them and have those boys back in no time, all set for the festivities." He tried to sound cheerful, but everyone could hear the tinge of worry in his voice.

The people in the small auditorium were nervous. There were hundreds of years of history in the small Cape Cod town, and missing people had happened before. In fact, there were stories that circulated now and then saying that every fifty years, a group of townspeople went missing and were never found - or so the legends went.

As the constable rounded up the adults present and gave assignments for each search area, ElsBeth was quietly moving toward the back door behind the stage. Before she got out, several girls of the class surrounded her. Veronica seemed to be the spokesperson. "El, we know you're going to look for them. Take us with you, we can help."

ElsBeth whispered back, "Quiet, you'll get their attention and none of us will be able to leave." Right or wrong, ElsBeth thought she could do better alone. But when she looked over the brave, anxious faces of her friends, she decided it wouldn't be fair to leave them.

So, making themselves very quiet and natural looking, one by one, Ms. Finch's second grade class, girls section, made its way beyond the maroon velvet stage curtain and slipped out the back.

ElsBeth led them quickly to the nearby wood where they wouldn't be seen. The girls huddled around ElsBeth. Some already had their Halloween costumes on, but it was too late to do anything about that.

"OK, what do we know? Constable Sylvester already asked, but think hard, did anyone see where the boys went after school?" Several small faces tightened up in concentration. Amy, looking fearful in her pink fairy costume, said, "Well, I saw two of them on their scooters hanging around town in the last week, but this morning I think I saw Jimmy take off on his bike on the road to the old lighthouse."

ElsBeth said, "Very good, Amy. Anyone else?"

Veronica said, "You know, I saw Robert Hillman-Jones in the Eastern Mountain Sports store in Hyannis last Saturday, and he was buying three sets of those headband flashlights and several collapsible sacks. Maybe that is a clue. I just thought he was over-preparing for Trick or Treating. You know Robert. But why would he buy *three* headlamps?"

"Right!" ElsBeth thought they were getting someplace now. "Good work, Veronica."

Suddenly ElsBeth's dream came back to her. Robert Hillman-Jones in the damp, and a pirate and his booty!

ElsBeth nearly shouted. "I know what they are doing! They are after Billy Bowlegs' hidden treasure!" But she caught herself just in time and whispered it instead.

The rest of the girls let out a gasp. They had all heard of Billy Bowlegs. Everyone in town had. In the 1700's Captain Billy was a notorious pirate who had preyed upon ships carrying Spanish gold. He was most known for his exploits around the Caribbean. But he had had a sweetheart, Verity Hope Hoxie, right here on Cape Cod.

The stories went that the pirate had brought all the gold back to the Cape as a wedding gift for Verity Hope. It was said that the treasure was hidden in a cave somewhere mid-Cape. It was part of the legend that there was a jealous rival for sweet Verity's hand, and when Captain Bowlegs and his men were hiding the gold, Verity Hope's other admirer, Captain Ebenezer Toothacher, had followed them into the secret cave. And in a fierce sword fight, all had been mortally wounded and the treasure and its location were lost forever.

It was said that both ghosts were restless - always searching for Verity Hope. And there were rumors that Captain Bowlegs still jealously guarded his treasure. Some said that the two didn't even know they were dead! And on rare lonely nights in October they could be heard arguing and clanking swords.

Other folks with more common sense (and less imagination) said it was "the wind blowing through the rigging" or "the waves on the buoys" or "chains holding the boats in the harbor" that made the noises. But when the chilling sounds came, as they always did on certain nights, anyone who heard them felt the shivers run up and down their spines.

Veronica was the first to recover. "Everyone knows that is just an old tale."

"Maybe," said ElsBeth. "But you know Hillman-Jones. Do you think that would stop him?"

Veronica thought about it and responded, "No, that would only make him more interested."

"Right," said ElsBeth. "They must think the gold is in the caves beyond the old lighthouse. We'll have to go there as quickly as we can."

Luckily everyone had on sturdy sneakers, as they had all prepared for maximum-speed Trick or Treating.

"Let's go!" And with that, the small band of girls took off, following the deer path through the woods that would take them toward the light house point and the mysterious caves beyond.

Chapter X
Hannah Goodspell Gets Involved

Back at the purple and pink Victorian on Druid Lane, Hannah Goodspell was listening attentively to Sylvanas who had witnessed the stir going on at the auditorium. The cat had subsequently eavesdropped to get the full details, as was his habit. He had all the news, and he quickly brought the witch up to date on the situation with the missing boys. He was not, however, yet aware that ElsBeth and her band of second grade girls had become involved in a secret rescue attempt of their own.

Hannah shook her head and briskly pulled off her apron. "My, my, so it happens once again." Hannah had been around during each of the preceding disappearances, and despite her magical efforts, she had not been able to find the townspeople who had gone missing.

This time, hearing it was a pack of young boys from ElsBeth's class, she was more determined than ever that they should be found safe and sound and returned to their families.

She quickly decided that the best strategy was to first get the local animals enlisted in the search. They could cover much more territory and were always wary of people. Boys, especially young boys, in their habitat, were always noticed. Hannah ruled out the village as the boys' hiding place. It would be almost impossible for a handful of them not to be noticed in town, particularly with all the Halloween activity going on today.

Sylvanas would round up the cats, including all the feral cats who would be the sharpest lookouts. He would brief them and put them on the alert.

Bartholomew, who had been nearby and listening attentively while Sylvanas imparted his shocking news, was quick to offer his help, as well. "I can get the marsh frogs, the field toads and at least some of the fish to help. I hope we get no answer from the fish though, as it could mean only the worst for the little boys if they fell into their domain," he croaked sadly.

An enormous blue heron, named Thaddeus Crane, a stately water bird who often visited the marsh behind Hannah's house, said he would enlist the help of the seabirds. He huffily added that, "The land birds would be of no assistance, being that they were all mindless creatures only interested in bugs, berries and the latest bird gossip."

Hannah thanked Thaddeus and described the pack of boys so that he could pass on the description to the eagles and ospreys, whose sharp eyes would be most needed in these dire circumstances.

Hannah would have liked to have enlisted the aid of the Cape deer and hare as well, but they were so skittish, she felt she couldn't afford the time it would take to approach them without scaring them off. She also couldn't ask the bats as it was now broad daylight and they would be completely blinded by the bright sun and of no use.

With the local animals now assisting in the search, Hannah decided to take her bicycle and visit the shaman of the Wampanoag next. He had his own friends among the creatures, and his people may have already heard something.

She quickly donned a large green hat and a tartan plaid cape from the Puritan shop. She then cast a simple speed spell on her bicycle, which leapt ahead just as she was jumping on - and with cape and hat flapping wildly, the older witch was off.

Chapter XI
The Girls Continue the Search

Meanwhile ElsBeth and the girls were halfway to the lighthouse.

By now some of the girls were getting a little nervous. Carmen was not so sure about going into a cave. "El, what if it is slimy? What if there are ... mice!" she cried with increasing alarm.

ElsBeth tried to calm her down. "You can stay outside. We'll need a lookout anyway."

Veronica on the other hand was completely poised. She had begun to daydream about being a hero and having her picture in the paper - maybe even on TV! She had just bought a new sweater and she could borrow her mother's gold necklace – the one with the shells set between polished beads of sea glass. With any luck she would look at least ten, almost a teenager!

ElsBeth could only concentrate on Robert Hillman-Jones and the rest of the boys. At least he had Johnny Twofeathers with him. Johnny was smart and an Indian, which meant he should have no small ability when it came to dealing with ghosts!

The girls had come to the marsh grass now and decided not to chance the road. The marsh grass was tall enough to easily hide them. After all, none of them were over four feet. They would have to be careful of the tide, but it was pretty low now. ElsBeth thought they could make it to the lighthouse before the marsh flooded and cut them off. But would they?

Chapter XII
Hannah Goodspell Enlists the Aid of the Indians

In no time at all Hannah had made it to the Legion Hall where Eddie "Wily" Coyote spent most of his days informally running local tribal affairs. The Legion Hall was almost completely dark, and most of the eyes that turned toward her were bright sparks in the shadows. She quickly spotted Eddie Coyote's deeply wrinkled face and went over to him.

"It is good to see you, my old friend. Greetings and best wishes," said Hannah. One needed to keep up one's manners, no matter how desperate the situation.

"I have some alarming news. It has happened again, my friend. A group from the town has gone missing."

Eddie Coyote looked at the witch closely. "What business is it of the tribe if foolish tourists get themselves lost and disappear?" he responded without much concern. "These ignorant outsiders often get lost or shipwrecked or killed with drink." It wasn't a subject that interested him much.

Hannah had to hold her temper in check at this indifference, but she couldn't help snapping back, "Well, this time it is a group of young boys from the town, and one of them is Johnny Twofeathers, grandson of Lester

Killfish and your great, great nephew, I believe." At this surprising announcement, Eddie Coyote stood up straight and said, "Johnny can be a little reckless, but he's not a fool. What is he doing with a pack of lost schoolboys?"

Hannah tried hard to keep the exasperation out of her voice. She needed his help. "I don't know, but we've got to find them before something happens."

Eddie Coyote at last seemed to see the dangerousness of the situation. Instead of leaping into action though, he abruptly went into a deep trance. The Indian wise man was so completely still that not even a hair on his head moved for what seemed like ages. But it was in reality only a matter of minutes before he suddenly slumped down into the chair. The old man shook himself, pulled his shoulders back and straightened up again. His face got serious and he told the witch with complete certainty, "They are after Billy Bowlegs."

Hannah did not question how he knew. Witches weren't the only ones with powers beyond the norm. With a shiver of fear, she recalled that everyone she had ever heard of over the centuries who went looking for Billy Bowlegs' pirate hoard had ended up either disappointed or had disappeared and was presumed... dead.

"We need to find them. Now!" she almost yelled. "Will you help?"

"Yes," the Medicine Man had decided. "If Johnny Twofeathers is with them, they will get close to the gold and they will need help.

"I'll get Pete Eaglesbeak to take his crop duster up for a look, and we'll get the men with fishing boats to check out the shoreline. It's too bad – they should leave Billy Bowlegs to his gold. That pirate will never give up his treasure. It has been well over two hundred years and no one has got it yet." He spat a wad of tobacco into the nearby brass spittoon and got up, ready for action at last.

Hannah left, knowing these Indians would be in the air and on the water in no time.

She had best get to the Town Library, quick as a wink, to find out all she could about Billy Bowlegs and the location of his hidden treasure. She had no idea where to start looking with all the miles of rugged coast nearby. When you needed to find out something related to the intricate history of Cape Cod, even if you were a witch, the Town Library was the place to be!

Chapter XIII
The Girls Get Close

By now it was mid-afternoon, storm clouds were rolling in, and the girls were getting exhausted. Amy's pixie costume had started to droop, the iridescent wings flapping slowly behind her. All the girls looked a little worse for wear. Fortunately Veronica had come with several Cadbury bars, which she had shared equally amongst all the girls. Each was able to have three small squares, which had kept them going so far.

One of the girls had been about to throw a wrapper into the marsh grass when ElsBeth gently stopped her and explained, "You must think of the creatures of the marsh. The fish and the birds will be attracted to the bright foil and will try to eat it, thinking it is a small silver fish, but their insides will get all torn up trying to digest it. We must never throw candy wrappers or any plastic away in nature. It can last practically forever, and it will hurt or kill any creatures who tangle with it or try to eat it - never mind how ugly it is to see trash in the woods or on the dunes or in the marshes," she added with a sad shake of her head.

Some of the girls looked at each other with guilty glances. ElsBeth's words struck home. They had never thought of that before when they had carelessly tossed things away.

They were all thinking about the poor creatures when Amy, who had somehow gotten into the lead, froze and abruptly stopped. Carmen who was close behind didn't notice and ran right into her, and Veronica stumbled, just barely avoiding Carmen in the process. The girls had been moving closer together and bunching up, the nearer they got to the lighthouse. When Amy stopped so quickly, the whole line of tired girls was jostled all around.

The lighthouse had just come into view and someone stage whispered, "I think I saw something move in the lighthouse."

The girls looked up immediately, but no one could see clearly. A thick fog was moving in fast, and the lighthouse had disappeared again.

"You, you ... couldn't have seen anything," stuttered Carmen, "That lighthouse has been abandoned for 50 years."

"Maybe that's where the boys are," whispered Veronica.

No one took a step.

"No," ElsBeth was firm. "They are in Billy Bowlegs' cave. I just know it."

"How are we going to find the cave if no one knows where it is?" piped up Lisa Lee. Lisa was wearing an overlarge witch's costume caked with marsh mud all along the bottom. Her large glasses kept slipping down her button nose, making her look like some bedraggled miniature witch professor. Lisa Lee almost never said anything, so the girls paid attention to her when she actually spoke up with this sensible question. Lisa was always logical, even if she was unnervingly quiet most of the time.

ElsBeth hadn't worked out how to find the cave yet, but she knew that if the boys had been seen on the road to the lighthouse, it must be nearby. There was nothing else out this way. The lighthouse road went for five miles to the rocky point and there were no side roads, there was only marsh land, then open water. The cave had to be somewhere on the rocky point. "Let's look for signs. Their bikes must be nearby. Knowing that Hillman-Jones was in charge, the boys would never have walked very far."

While the girls were talking, they had been closely approaching, then passing the old abandoned lighthouse. As they came around it on the ocean side, they stopped short and bumped into each other again. There were ten bicycles hidden hastily behind the structure and ditched any which way. But more mysterious than that was a jet black Range Rover with British license plates.

Veronica spoke up first. "I've seen that SUV around town in the last week or two, but I don't know who it belongs to. What would tourists be doing out here?"

Carmen whispered, "Maybe it's not tourists, maybe it's treasure hunters and they've got the boys and...." Carmen's lower lip began to quiver and tears filled up her soft, dark eyes.

The girls became even more frightened at this latest idea.

"Poor Nelson," cried Amy, "I never should have made fun of his ears."

"Pull yourself together, Amy," snapped Veronica.

ElsBeth tried to remain calm. After all, she was a witch. No matter what the situation was, she would deal with it. "We mustn't panic. We're smarter than the boys, and even if they are captured, we'll figure out a way to get them out...alive. We just have to find them first."

"Girls, from here on out we have to be quiet as field mice. We need to assess the situation and come up with a plan. No crying or loud noises. We are going to find them. Now follow me." ElsBeth bravely led the girls to the rock outcrops. No one saw anything though, except for rocks, and more rocks. Occasionally a spotted seal would swim by, his sleek head popping up and then circling back.

Finally the seal's bark got through to ElsBeth. In all the excitement she had again forgotten the most important thing. She was a witch, and she could communicate with all the creatures around if she would only listen and pay attention. The seal must have seen something, and he would help her and her friends to find their classmates. ElsBeth couldn't very well start barking like a seal in front of her friends, so she sent a vivid mental projection of the boys' images in the seal's direction. The seal barked back a little impatiently, "That's what I've been trying to tell you! They are in the cave, but bad men are with them and they have weapons. You must be very careful. Better yet, go back and get help!" He hastily added an introduction, "Sam Seal at your service, young witch."

ElsBeth was fearful. She couldn't bring her friends into such danger. "Girls, go back to the lighthouse. I've got an idea where they are now. I'll find them and bring them back."

The girls tried to argue with her, but she used her witch's skill and enchanted them a little with a lilting voice. (It didn't count as a spell.) One by one they reluctantly turned and headed back to the lighthouse.

Sam Seal said, "Well, witch, I guess you are determined to find them. Just remember, many a soul has searched for Billy Bowlegs' treasure, but none who've found it have ever returned to tell the tale."

At this, ElsBeth gulped and stuck her chin up. "Surely none of them were witches." She barked back her answer in the seal's own language, now that her classmates weren't around to hear.

"True enough, true enough. Follow me, little one." Sam Seal swam slowly next to the rocky shore, while ElsBeth scrambled to keep up with him. The seal was solemn, as he led ElsBeth closer and closer to mortal danger.

Finally they came alongside an opening half hidden by the rocks. It was now partially underwater as the tide had just turned.

Sam Seal stopped and nodded silently at the opening. ElsBeth gulped again. She felt in her pocket for her orange, pumpkin flashlight and resolutely headed for the entrance, which was narrowing minute by minute with the tide.

Chapter XIV
Hannah Researches the Pirate

Meanwhile, back at the crammed town archives section of the library, Hannah was making alarming discoveries of her own.

Beginning in the 1700's, there were accounts of the notorious pirate, Billy Bowlegs, and his band of cutthroats. Apparently his one and only soft spot had been his love for his Cape Cod sweetheart Verity Hope.

The records stated that he'd hidden the hoard he had accumulated during years of plundering the rich Spanish galleons on the Southern seas somewhere near his sweetheart's home in Harwich Center. In several town reports it was hinted that there was a cave near the ocean that was crammed full of gold and silver and jewels, the spoils of the pirate's many successful robberies on the high seas. But it was noted to be cleverly hidden.

In the hundreds of years since his sudden disappearance, along with that of his rival for Verity Hope's affections, many had looked, but no one had ever found so much as a single gold coin. That is – no one had ever found the treasure and had returned to tell about it.

Apparently five separate times, groups of men had gone in search of the pirate's booty and each time the party had disappeared without a trace, never to be seen or heard from again. Since Hannah had moved from Salem all those years ago, she'd heard stories of the treasure but had never had the time to pay enough attention. Pirate gold was fine but she was a witch and had much more important things to worry about - the crops, the weather, the catch for the fisherman, the lives of the village people. Gold and jewels were just not important to a good witch. Several of these times she had begun to help when men were lost, but each time she'd always found her hands full preventing some other local catastrophe, so she'd never actually gotten completely involved in one of those searches...until now.

There were many old maps in the archives that tried to pinpoint Billy Bowlegs' treasure trove. Taken collectively there were X marks all along the local coast, and several inland as well. That wasn't any help in narrowing it down. "Well, it doesn't appear the answer is here after all," Hannah muttered to herself.

Just as she was about to close the last faded old calfskin scroll, she heard a shout and saw a commotion out the library window.

Sylvanas popped up on the granite sill a second later.

"ElsBeth and the rest of the second grade girls are missing, too. They must have gone in search of the boys," he spat out. Sylvanas, normally the most snide and aloof of felines, appeared genuinely angry and even a little afraid underneath. "ElsBeth's a good enough witch to find them, but she's not experienced enough to get them out of any trouble they've managed. And my feral cat troops report trouble brewing with a capital T," he continued.

Hannah asked him to quickly bring her up to speed - "I've checked all the maps and there are just too many places they could be."

By now Sylvanas had gathered important information. "Several feral cats saw the boys heading toward the old abandoned lighthouse around dawn. There is nothing else out that way. But none of these ignorant cats had the sense to follow them or got close enough to eavesdrop – lazy creatures. ElsBeth and the girls were spotted several hours later headed in the same direction. They were taking the deer path through the marshes so they wouldn't be seen. Again, those brainless kittens didn't think to follow them. I'll have one of their nine lives each for this!"

Sylvanas was spitting mad to be let down so by his brethren.

Just then, an exceptionally large osprey, circling above, cried loudly, catching their attention. "The girls are safe by the lighthouse. All but ElsBeth have been spotted. But there is a strange black vehicle parked there, the windows are tinted and even my sharp eyes can't see inside to check for the boys."

Hannah and Sylvanas wasted no time. Hannah stepped on her bicycle, muttered another speed spell, and whirled down the cobblestone road with Sylvanas riding in the wicker basket, sphinx-like in his favorite pose, and managing to look regal, despite the dire emergency - and the bumps.

Meanwhile the Wampanoags, using their own methods, had come to the same conclusion, and at this very moment several small fishing boats were also converging on the abandoned lighthouse.

Chapter XV
Adventure in the Pirate Cave

ElsBeth had not turned on her flashlight yet. She had squeezed herself in as close to the side of the cave as she could. The entrance was an extremely long narrow opening, which turned a corner at the end. And there was some feeble light emanating from just past the turn. She could just hear muttered whispering, but the voices sounded far too deep for Robert Hillman-Jones and the other second grade boys.

She began again after getting her bearings and was heading slowly toward the bend, careful not to splash in the puddle that was starting to deepen on the cave floor. As she went, she was surprised to realize that she could see rather well. Then she heard Professor Badinoff, her familiar, squeaking out a greeting. He quickly added instructions, "Don't use your eyes. You must rely on your hearing and sonar."

ElsBeth hadn't realized she even had sonar, but she tried sending out a little beam and found she could perceive when it hit the wall and bounced back. In fact, when she thought she was "seeing", she had actually been using sonar without even thinking about it. "Wow, thanks, Professor!" she squeaked back to her friend.

"Don't use your flashlight - there are some bad men ahead. They have the boys captured. ElsBeth, be careful, they have guns!" he squeaked in batspeak.

As ElsBeth watched Professor Badinoff fly ahead, a hand reached out of the dark suddenly and closed over ElsBeth's mouth. The small witch was so scared she almost fainted.

Then Johnny Twofeathers's round head popped up right in front of her face, and he was attached to the hand covering her mouth! ElsBeth immediately slumped forward in relief and would have spoken out loud, but Johnny Twofeathers made the silence sign by drawing a finger over his lips and pointed towards the bend. He then slowly released her. ElsBeth took a deep breath. She was so happy to see her friend.

Johnny used Indian sign language and signaled silently to ElsBeth what had happened. Johnny explained that Robert Hillman-Jones had overheard some strangers talking about pirate treasure. He and the boys had been following them for several weeks every chance they could get. The boys had been organized to take turns spying on the men after school and on the weekends.

Yesterday, the strangers thought they had found something, so Robert Hillman-Jones decided they would all have to follow them today. In the diner the men were overheard whispering about the old lighthouse, so the boys made sure they were at the lighthouse just after dawn before the strangers would arrive this morning. They had then followed the strangers into the cave around noontime.

Johnny Twofeathers had been taking up the rear as lookout when something went wrong. Nelson Hamm had tripped over some loose rocks and the men were alerted, and they came to the cave entrance with guns. All the boys had been roughly herded into the cave. But Johnny, who'd been behind, managed to slip back unnoticed. He had hidden outside the cave hoping to hear something and come up with a rescue plan. He had finally decided to go back into the cave just before ElsBeth had come along.

"I'll go first," Johnny signed to ElsBeth, and then added unnecessarily, "Be quiet."

ElsBeth bit her tongue and bravely followed. It was up to her and Johnny to rescue their friends.

The two crept closer and closer to the bend until they were able to peek into the cavern one at a time.

They saw huge blackened beams and large chunks of granite rock that had been placed to shore up the natural chamber. A smaller cavern could just be made out. It opened up just beyond the large chamber. Towards the end of the first one, were two men. They were big and held large pistols. Both were dressed in LL Bean hiking clothes, and had binoculars around their necks. One of them had a Petersen bird guide sticking out of his pocket.

ElsBeth wondered why bird watchers would be carrying guns and searching for pirate treasure, but it quickly dawned on her that it was a simple disguise. They were trying to look like tourists.

Nearby, all the second grade boys were huddled together in a corner looking wet and frightened.

One of the men was speaking, "Well, what should we do with the little blighters?" He sounded a little like a pirate himself.

The other one looked something like Dr. Doolittle and spoke in a refined, upper-class,

British accent. He responded, "Nothing. All the legends say no one ever returned alive after looking for Billy Bowlegs' treasure. We'll just make sure they are here at high tide and get washed to sea. Let's let Billy Bowlegs' curse and Father Neptune do our dirty work for us. It will be another tragic accident." He added with a nasty little laugh, "Now, help me lift the trapdoor."

ElsBeth and Johnny Twofeathers watched in fascination as the two men began to haul on a tarnished old brass ring attached to the heavy oaken trap door, set firmly into the floor of the cave.

ElsBeth's mind was whirling trying to come up with a plan to divert the men's attention long enough to let the boys escape.

Suddenly the men's persistent tugging paid off and the trapdoor came loose with a great sound of sucking mud letting go - it was a terribly rude sound, and ElsBeth stifled the hysterical giggles that threatened to come out.

The refined one in the teal and navy polypro pullover grabbed his flashlight, looking like a mad spelunker for a moment. When the light flashed in the sub cavern, thousands of sparkles winked back. There were broken chests of gold and glittering jewels. The silver had turned black with age, so much so that it appeared that amidst the bright, shiny treasure there were the deepest, black holes, completely devoid of any light.

Though you couldn't tell in the cave, it was almost dusk now - a witching hour in any case - but all the more potent, as it was that most special, mystical night where the natural world and the spirit world were closest - Halloween.

ElsBeth suddenly felt a shift in the natural world and it was no longer a cave with age blackened beams. The wood was new, just like when it was originally put in place, back in the 1700's. The men were gleefully seeing nothing but the treasure. But even they shifted nervously for a moment. The one of them that looked like a pirate lifted a blackened silver box to his face and began to open it. Just then, from behind him, a loud swoosh cut through the air!

There was Billy Bowlegs, in the flesh so to speak. Well, not quite "flesh", but clearly it once was. He had a huge curved sword called a cutlass in outstretched hands. He wasn't very tall, but he was wide and mean looking and totally scary, balanced on his wide bow legs.

The pirate laughed out in a booming voice, "Billy Bowlegs 'ere. Pleased to make yer acquaintance. I always like to be polite 'afore I cut a man's 'ead off!" He swaggered towards the men.

Before they had a chance to react, one of them screamed at the top of his lungs, sounding surprisingly like Carmen seeing a mouse. He dropped the silver box he had been holding, and started swatting at what looked like two extremely angry humming birds buzzing around his head.

ElsBeth whispered, "Fairies. It is the two fairies Grandmother spoke of!"

The fairies, having excellent hearing, flew right over to investigate ElsBeth. "Definitely a witch," said the one with the darker wings. The other added, "Let's save it. It's cute!"

ElsBeth didn't know what to think, but before she had time to respond, shots were ringing out toward the back of the cave.

The men were fighting fiercely with Billy Bowlegs for his awesome treasure. The boys in the corner huddled closer, stiff with fear.

Johnny Twofeathers grabbed ElsBeth and pulled her towards the boys. "Now's our chance. Come on. Let's get them out of here."

ElsBeth and Johnny, followed by the two fairies and the huge bat, dashed to the boys and started pulling and pushing them to their feet. The boys were nearly frozen with the cold and terror but they quickly got themselves together.

Robert Hillman-Jones looked up in surprise and said, "ElsBeth, you can't be here!" then fainted dead away. Nelson and Frankie Sylvester grabbed his legs, and Johnny and ElsBeth picked him up by the arms, and they all started stumbling back toward the entrance.

Billy Bowlegs stopped mid sword sweep and yelled, "Arrrgh. They're escaping!" and began to take off after the children. This made the prickly fairies angry as they had decided on the spot to adopt ElsBeth and her friends. They buzzed right up to the old pirate and started spinning around his head. Their iridescent wings beat so fast that all the pirate could see was a sparkling blur in front of him. "Damn my eyes!" he yelled while trying to poke at the fairies with his sword.

The two Englishmen took this opportunity to try to escape, grabbing as much loot as they could carry. But suddenly there was a moving slimy wall of frogs in front of them, bravely led by Bartholomew, and all they could do was slip and slide.

The fairies tired quickly of taunting the old pirate and also headed for the treasure hunters. With their extremely sharp teeth, they began to nip at the men's ears. "Ow! Ow!" the men screamed.

By now the children had almost made the entrance. Nelson had dropped Hillman-Jones' legs a couple of times, so one of the other boys took over. Nelson's strength began to flag and he fell behind the others.

At the front now, Frankie Sylvester screamed, "Indians!" and dodged back into the cave. At that, Johnny Twofeathers and ElsBeth dropped Hillman-Jones altogether and ran to the front of the entrance.

It was quite a sight that met them. There was a long canoe with two young Indians in what looked like war paint, but was really hunting camouflage they hadn't had time to wipe off when they'd been called to the search by Eddie Coyote's alert. They were holding whale harpoons and had on florescent orange hunting caps.

Hovering to the east was an ocean kayak led by Sam Seal and a few members of his court. Several strong Indians in waders were guarding the entrance to the cave with spiked fishing spears. Behind them were a small dingy with a ten horse outboard motor and an old fishing trawler.

In the prow of the dingy, looking majestic while carefully keeping every single cat hair as far away from the water as possible, was Sylvanas, and right behind him was Hannah. A thought crossed ElsBeth's mind that the cat looked like a cross between a mad hedgehog and a puma with all that black hair sticking straight up.

Johnny and ElsBeth smiled and began to wave their arms in the air, just as another shot rang out behind them.

Boys started pushing through the entrance and plopping into the water. Somehow frogs and toads were everywhere. ElsBeth and Johnny pushed Robert Hillman-Jones onto a rock, and Sam Seal took over keeping him from slipping into the sea, juggling his head out of the water like a small bouncing ball.

Someone yelled out, "Where's Nelson?   He was right behind me."

ElsBeth and Johnny Twofeathers darted back into the cave, which was rapidly filling up now as the tide came in.

More shots rang out. Professor Badinoff flew by ElsBeth's head and squeaked out, "Back there. Nelson's down."

Cautiously they headed back into the cavern. Billy Bowlegs, looking thinner and wispier than before, was fighting the two Englishmen, who by now had several bleeding cuts. Their ears were bright red with fairy bites. They were fighting over the trap door, with the gold, and glittering diamonds, rubies, emeralds and pearls again lighting them from below.

With the force of the incoming tide, Nelson had floated back towards the fracas. He was breathing, but his arm was at a funny angle and there was blood....

"We've got to save him," cried Johnny. "ElsBeth, I know you're a witch. Do something ... witchy."

ElsBeth was so surprised that she dropped the pumpkin flashlight she'd been holding to light the way in this time. At the noise, both the pirate and the men had a new target.

There was no time to think. There was no time for permission. There was no time! ElsBeth closed her eyes in concentration and her voice rang out, filling the cave with a powerful spell:

> "Birds of the air;
> Creatures of the sea;
>   Wind and water;
> Come to ME!"

Suddenly a huge wave crashed into the cavern, knocking over ElsBeth, Johnny and the Englishmen.

Billy Bowlegs just yelled, "Shiver me timbers!" and slashed again at the two men with his sword.

The wave pushed ElsBeth and Johnny right beside Nelson. "Grab his head!" Johnny yelled over the surf. ElsBeth and Johnny started struggling with Nelson's dead weight as a great flock of birds and bats flew into the cave and a huge shark swam past them.

"Quick – Out, now!" screamed Johnny.

A blast of wind came up and the three children were blown clear to the front of the cave. Screeching and screaming rose to a fever pitch behind them.

A huge storm was brewing on the horizon. They needed to get out fast. The boats wouldn't be able to stay out in this weather, and the rocks at the entrance were being battered with huge waves.

ElsBeth and Johnny were rapidly tiring from pulling Nelson. And Nelson started saying funny things as if he were delirious. It began to look bleak for the three remaining classmates; they weren't going to make it after all. Then suddenly at the final moment they felt strong hands pull them up into the safety of the ocean kayak.

The last thing ElsBeth saw before she passed out from exhaustion was her grandmother and Sylvanas sailing by, heading for the cave at full speed driven by tribal elder, Eddie "Wily" Coyote, and led by Sam Seal.

Chapter XVI
Back on Main Street

The Halloween celebrations had been cancelled, but everyone in the town was so relieved that the children were back safely that no one complained.

All the children were gathered around Nelson's bed in Old Doc Mather's infirmary on Cohoag Drive. Nelson had had his arm set in a handsome electric blue cast, and was sitting up now, looking pale, but smiling dazedly. Amy, her fairy wings still drooping, was sitting in a small rocking chair by his side and holding his hand.

Robert Hillman-Jones, in the next bed, was sitting up and boasting about how they would go back and claim the treasure, when Hannah and Sylvanas entered the room.

"What treasure?" she sang out in a musical voice, so enchanting that all around felt they must be dreaming. "Pirates and golden treasure are legends surely," she lilted. Everyone felt very pleasant listening to Hannah, very relaxed. "The boys got lost by the old lighthouse and found an old cave. They were trapped when the tide came in and the Indians rescued them. Boys always look for treasure, but that's just an old story. Nothing more."

They all were nodding their heads in agreement.

Robert Hillman-Jones tried to shake it off, but eventually he started nodding, too.

Hannah then brightly announced, "It's Halloween!" And the spell was broken. "The teachers have brought the party here!"

And there at the door was Ms. Finch dressed in shiny emerald green, looking like either an iridescent grasshopper or a large preying mantis. It wasn't really clear. But she was smiling and carrying a lobster pot filled with candy.

The Constable muscled in a barrel for apple bobbing and began filling it up with water. The rest of the teachers brought Halloween decorations and started putting them on the blank walls.

Outside the window, those that couldn't fit into Doc's infirmary had started their own celebration going.

It was, hands down, turning into the best Halloween ever after all.

ElsBeth was in the corner eating chocolate that was rapidly spreading all over her face like some horrible skin disease. Johnny Twofeathers was sitting next to her. The only difference was his chocolate was going into his mouth without miscalculation, so his face was clean - Johnny had always been much neater than ElsBeth.

After a while ElsBeth turned to Johnny and said, "Chief, remember what you said in the cave?"

Johnny looked back at her blankly. "No. What did I say, ElsBeth?"

ElsBeth smiled happily. "Oh. Nothing important."

Chapter XVII
Witch House on Druid Lane

Back at home later that night, ElsBeth got up her nerve and said, "Grandmother, I have a confession to make."

Grandmother was tucking ElsBeth into her snug captain's bed with her puffy blue, half-moon comforter. "What is it, dear?"

"Well, er... well er... you know I was never, ever, ever, under any circumstances, to use witchery unless you were directly supervising me."

"Yes, ElsBeth," her grandmother looked grave.

"Er... today in the cave, er..., I did it," ElsBeth blurted out.

"Well, dear, you'll find out that there are rare times when the right thing to do is to break the rules. But I was right there and you did just fine," Hannah beamed down on her little witch.

ElsBeth smiled back, half asleep now. "Grandmother, what will happen to Billy Bowlegs and his treasure?"

Grandmother replied, "Only you and the boys are left who ever actually saw the pirate and the treasure, and the boys have already forgotten.

"The cave is now underwater again, and will be for another 50 years before the tides are just right to allow entrance. I imagine the deal I struck with Billy Bowlegs will keep. He gets to have his treasure secret and all to himself for the next 50 years, and then when it's a full moon, and Halloween, and the tides are just right, maybe a treasure hunter will come along and dare to match wits and courage with the famous pirate again. He quite enjoys it, you know."

ElsBeth was drifting. She was thinking of pirates and gold, of frogs and bats and talking seals.

She smiled dreamily. Life was certainly grand and full of adventure for the littlest witch on Cape Cod.

ElsBeth's Further Adventures

Things may have settled down for now in the small town on Cape Cod where ElsBeth and her friends are growing up, but that's bound to change in no time.

Be sure to keep an eagle eye out for ElsBeth and her friends. More adventures are clearly forecast for these particular young people. You can't keep a healthy bunch of Cape Cod kids out of trouble all the time!

Hannah Goodspell's gazing ball shows that before too long, ElsBeth and her friends will have a visit to her cousin's Scottish Castle – no doubt they'll be encountering a ghost or two there.

And what about the school trip to the Big Apple? What happens to them in the museum?

Then there's something about the hinterlands of China. But wait! We get ahead of ourselves.

I guess we'll have to be patient to find out what's next.

About the Author

J Bean Palmer has an abiding appreciation of the colorful history and breathtaking natural beauty of New England. This grew from her adventures flying small planes, hiking, canoeing and motorcycling in the rugged western mountains of Maine and the stunning seascapes and quaint villages of Cape Cod, where she and her husband now live. With a degree in Environmental Science from the University of Maine she believes passionately in the intelligent husbandry of our precious natural resources.

In *The Cape Cod Witch and the Pirate's Treasure,* the author also calls upon her family's long New England background, including a Revolutionary "Green Mountain Boy" and an oft-told family legend that as her grandmother's ancestors stepped off the

Mayflower, her grandfather's relatives were there to greet them.

She hopes to share some of this history and inspiration with her readers in this whimsical adventure set in the lyrical land of Cape Cod.

The author may be contacted by email at: jbeanpalmer@yahoo.com

About the Illustrator

Melanie Therrien lives in western Maine with her husband Glenn, stepson Dylon, their dog Sophie and their three cats, one of which was the model for Sylvanas in the ElsBeth story.

The Maine juried artist looks to the natural beauty in the state for inspiration for her fanciful flowers, butterflies and landscapes. She enjoys creating imaginary worlds and interesting characters in her preferred medium of acrylics. The stylistic artwork for *The Cape Cod Witch and the Pirate's Treasure* are her first book illustrations.

The artist may be contacted by email at therrien6@verizon.net

CAPE COD
NATIONAL OFFSET AND BINDERY, INC.

Printing by

Cape Cod National Offset & Bindery, Inc.
11 Jonathan Bourne Drive, Unit 3
Pocasset, MA 02559
Contact: Paul Petrie, Account Executive/Estimator
Tel: 508-563-5001 / Fax: 508-563-5002
paul.ccnationaloffset@comcast.net